WOLFF

Umschlag (Photo: Gerrit Engel) und
graphische Realisierung von Sergio Vitale
Gesamtherstellung: FotoLitho Longo
ISBN 3-89656-033-6
Printed in Italy

Bitte fordern Sie unser Gesamtverzeichnis an.
Write for our free catalogue:
Querverlag GmbH, Akazienstraße 25, D-10823 Berlin
http://www.querverlag.de

WOLFF

When we come into this world, we're naked. And when they cut the umbilical cord, we're suddenly on our own. Two things in our lives should be as natural and easy as possible: our nakedness and our autonomy. That's the way I live my life – a life full of wonder, adventure, and surprises. Thanks to everyone for your support – and a special thanks to all the photographers who have presented their views of Wolff.

Wenn wir geboren werden, sind wir nackt. Und wenn sie uns die Nabelschnur durchtrennen, sind wir plötzlich auf uns selbst gestellt. Es gibt also im Leben zwei Dinge, die natürlich und selbstverständlich sein sollten: unsere Nacktheit und unsere Autonomie. So führe ich mein Leben – ein Leben voller Wunder, Abenteuer und Überraschungen. Ich danke euch allen für eure Unterstützung – und ein besonderer Dank gilt den PhotographInnen, die hier ihre Sicht auf Wolff präsentieren.

Holger Zill alias 'Wolff'

Maja WOLFF

When you consider that Wolff makes his living doing porn movies, it was very endearing to discover, during the shoot, that he's actually a very shy person. At least at first.

Wenn man bedenkt, daß Wolff sein Geld mit Pornofilmen macht, fand ich es sehr charmant, daß er beim Shoot so schüchtern war. Am Anfang zumindest.

Maja

Born in Berlin in 1973, Maja Sara Rieck worked in several studios in Berlin and Hamburg from 1990 until 1996 before becoming a freelance photographer for a variety of magazines such as *Bravo*, *Spiegel*, *Style* and *Gala*, as well as for stage and music productions. In 1996, her work was exhibited in a show titled "Snapshot." She was the official photographer of the 1998 Love Parade in Berlin. Maja would like to thank Jonny Pazzo for the make-up and styling during the shoot.

Maja Sara Rieck, geboren 1973 in Berlin, arbeitete zwischen 1990 und 1996 in einigen Studios in Hamburg und Berlin, bevor sie sich selbständig machte. Seitdem arbeitet sie für Zeitschriften, z.B. *Bravo*, *Spiegel*, *Style* und *Gala*, und für Theater- und Musikveranstaltungen. 1996 fand eine Ausstellung ihrer Photographien unter dem Titel „Snapshot" statt. Darüber hinaus war sie 1998 die offizielle Photographin der Love Parade in Berlin. Maja bedankt sich bei Jonny Pazzo für Make-up und Styling während der Arbeit mit Wolff.

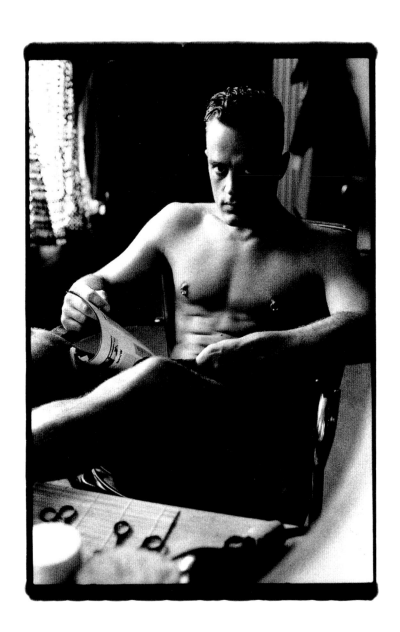

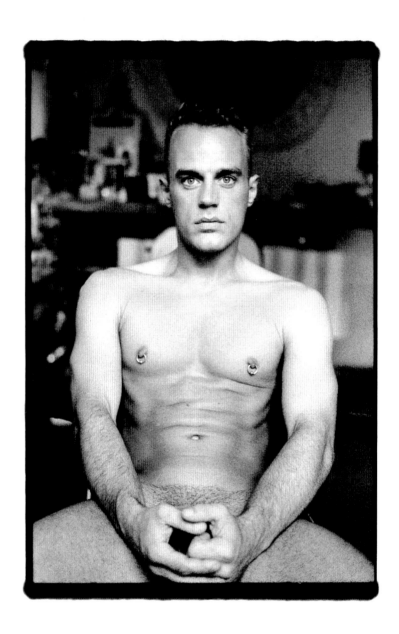

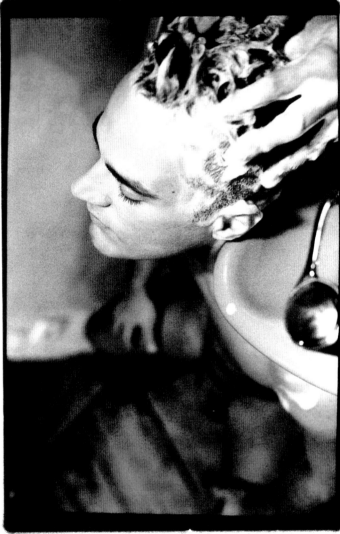

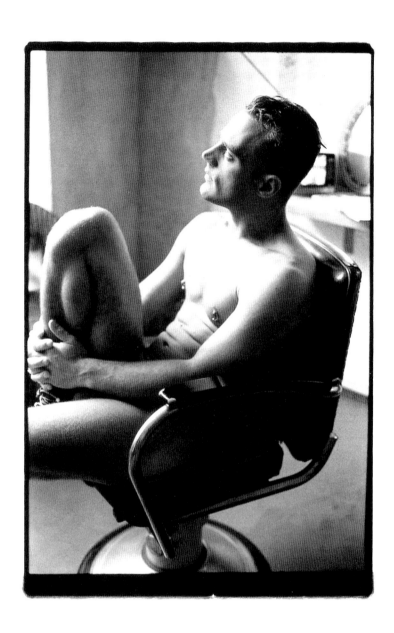

Christiane Pausch
WOLFF

"And now your underwear."
"What underwear?"

„Und jetzt der Schlüpfer."
„Welchen Schlüpfer denn?"

Christiane Pausch

Born in 1960 in Marburg/Lahn,
Christiane Pausch studied portrait
photography in Frankenberg before
working for Sender Freies Berlin. She
has been a freelance photographer
since 1992, specializing in television
and film productions. She lives with
her girlfriend in Berlin, has no house
pets, drinks, smokes and even eats red
meat. Her hobbies include motor-
cycling and camping. Her motto:
"Move closer to the lens!"

geboren 1960 in Marburg/Lahn,
studierte Porträtphotographie in
Frankenberg, danach arbeitete sie
beim Sender Freies Berlin. 1992
machte sie sich selbständig und ist
hauptsächlich im Bereich Film- und
Standphotographie tätig. Sie lebt fest
befreundet und ohne Haustiere in
Berlin/Kreuzberg, trinkt, raucht und
ißt Fleisch. Ihre Hobbys sind
Motorradfahren und Camping. Ihr
Motto: „Ran ans Motiv!"

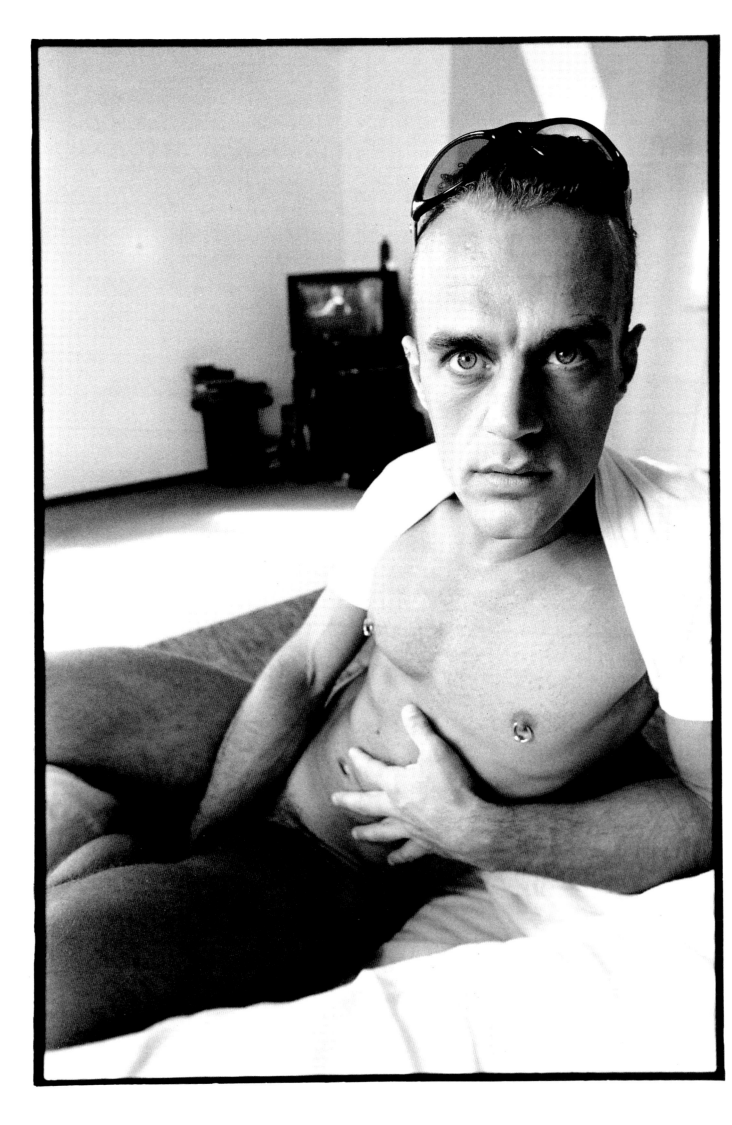

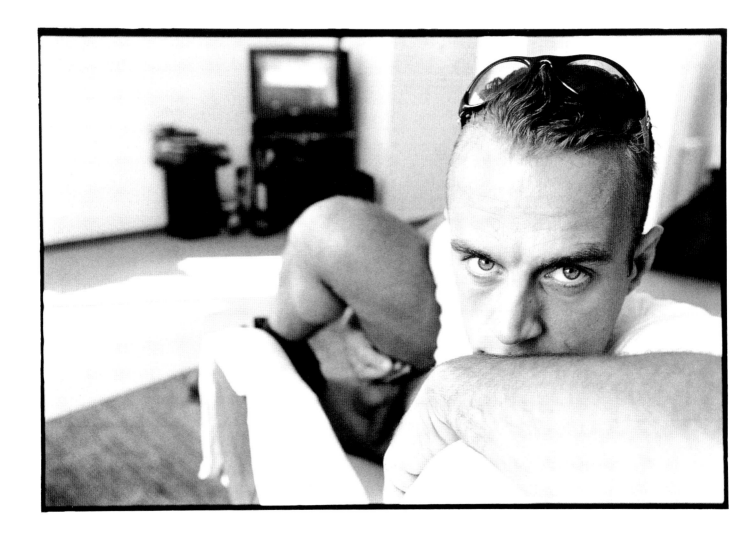

J.B. Higgins

WOLFF

I was struck by Wolff's physical presence, natural charm, and intelligence. He understood the artistic process – that search for the perfect moment when everything comes together. I thank the universe for allowing me the opportunity to be a part of that unexpected flow of creative energy.

An Wolff fiel mir gleich auf, wie körperbewußt, charmant und intelligent er ist. Er begriff den künstlerischen Akt sofort: diese Suche nach dem richtigen Moment, wenn alles zusammenkommt. Ich danke dem Universum, daß ich die Chance hatte, an dieser unerwarteten, kreativen Energie teilzuhaben.

' Self Postrait as *Fallen Angel* '   JBHiggins '98

J.B. Higgins

Born and raised in Kentucky, for the past 15 years J.B. Higgins has been living in San Francisco, where he works as a freelance photographer. He often uses the male nude to off-center the male icon in gay consciousness, thereby setting the stage to create fresh insight. His photography is and always will be a work in progress.

geboren in Kentucky. lebt seit 15 Jahren in San Francisco, wo er als freischaffender Photograph arbeitet. Er benutzt Aktphotographie, um die männliche Ikonographie im schwulen Bewußtsein zu unterminieren, und schafft dadurch neue Perspektiven. Seine Photographie ist und wird immer im Entstehen begriffen sein.

'Jesus of Berlin'   'Zill'   AB Higgins

kingdome 19

WOLFF

Wolff, thanks for your naturalness, your bareness, and your firmness.

Wolff, ich bedanke mich dafür, daß du so natürlich nackt und straff bist.

kíngdome 19 ———————————

Born 1966 in Berlin, kingdome 19 began his career as a landscape photographer before concentrating his efforts on the essentials: people. In his pursuit of more than simple portraits, he combines photography with graphic arts and creates unique, individual works of art. Besides providing cover art for CDs, film posters, and catalogues, he has worked with designers on fashion photography and has presented his work in several exhibits. kingdome 19 has also published two books of male photography: Euros Edition 7 – *kingdome 19* (1997) and kingdome 19 – *2OMEN* (1998).
Contact: kingdome 19, P.O. Box 4, 13161 Berlin, kingdome19@aol.com

geboren 1966 in Berlin, begann mit Landschaftsaufnahmen, doch bald zog ihn die Photographie zum Wesentlichen: dem Menschen. Er sucht mehr als nur die puren Aufnahmen; er vereint zwei Aspekte: Photographie und Graphik. Dadurch schafft er einzigartige Kunstwerke, Unikate. Darüber hinaus machte er mehrere Ausstellungen, erstellte Titelbilder für CDs, Filmfeste und Kataloge, und in Zusammenarbeit mit Designern betätigte er sich auch in der Modephotographie. 1997 veröffentlichte er sein erstes Buch: Euros Edition 7 – *kingdome 19*; 1998 folgte kingdome 19 – *2OMEN*.
Kontakt: kingdome 19, P.O. Box 4, 13161 Berlin, kingdome19@aol.com

UP AGAINST IT

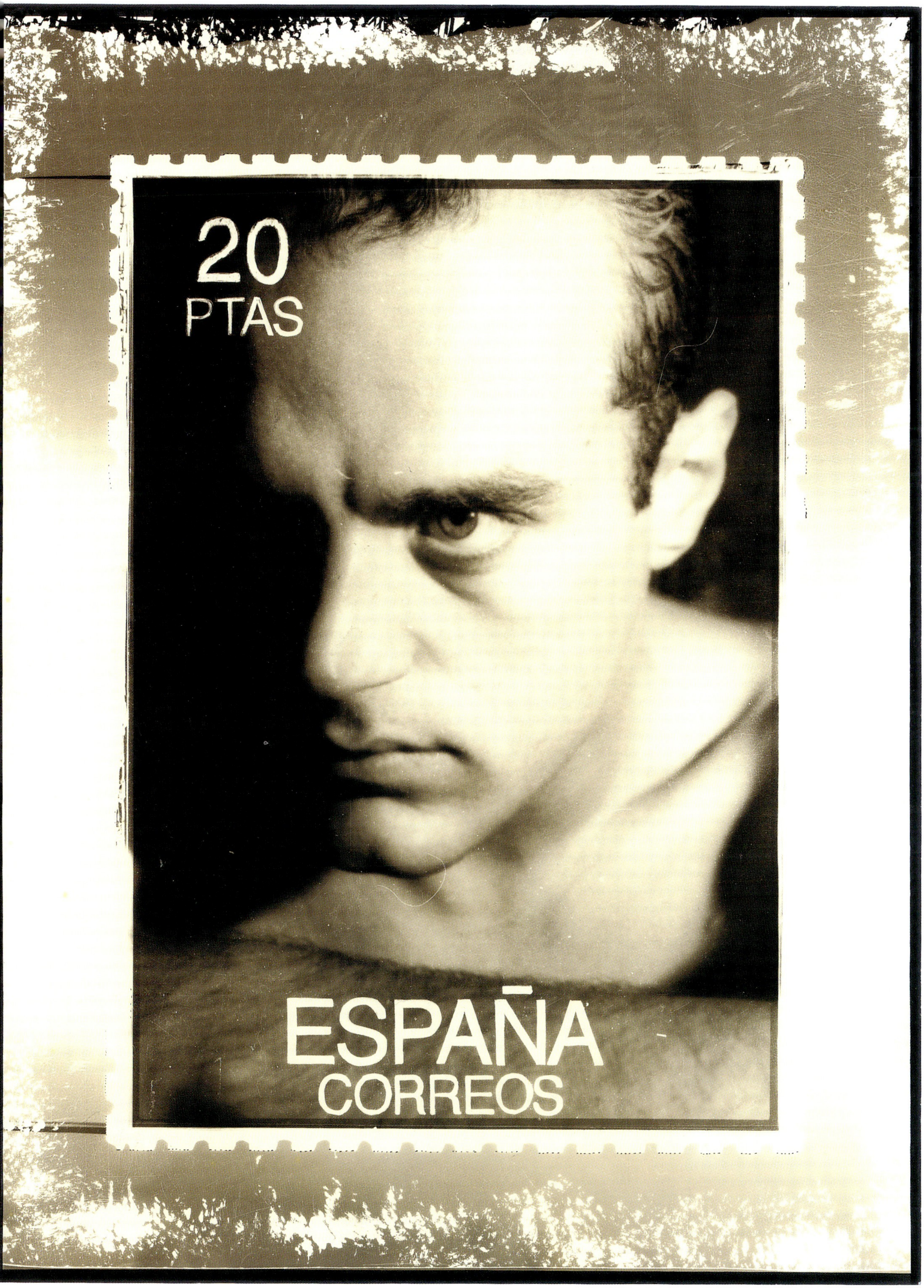
20
PTAS
ESPAÑA
CORREOS

Gerrit Engel
WOLFF

When I was asked to photograph Wolff, my first thought was to
refuse since I have never had much interest in nude photography.
But I was much too curious to work with someone who is so aware
of his body and knows how to use it as his capital asset. A big
thanks to everyone involved in this project – especially to Wolff!

Als ich gefragt wurde, Wolff zu photographieren, dachte ich zuerst
daran, abzulehnen, da Aktphotographie mich bisher nie
besonders interessiert hatte. Doch überwog letztendlich die
Neugier mit jemandem zu arbeiten, der so körperbewußt ist wie
Wolff. Einen herzlichen Dank an alle am Projekt Beteiligten –
und vor allem an Wolff!

Gerrit Engel

Born in 1965, Gerrit Engel studied
architecture and photography in
Munich and New York. Focussing on
architectural topics, he completed his
first book *Buffalo Grain Elevators* in
1997. He is currently working on a
book project on an East German
housing complex entitled *Marzahn*
juxtaposing architectural photography
with portraiture.

geboren 1965, studierte Architektur
und Photographie in München und
New York. Sich bisher hauptsächlich
Architekturthemen widmend, erschien
1997 das Buch *Buffalo Grain Elevators*.
In seinem neuen Band *Marzahn* über
das gleichnamige Ost-Berliner
Wohngebiet verbindet er
Architekturphotographie mit Porträt-
aufnahmen.

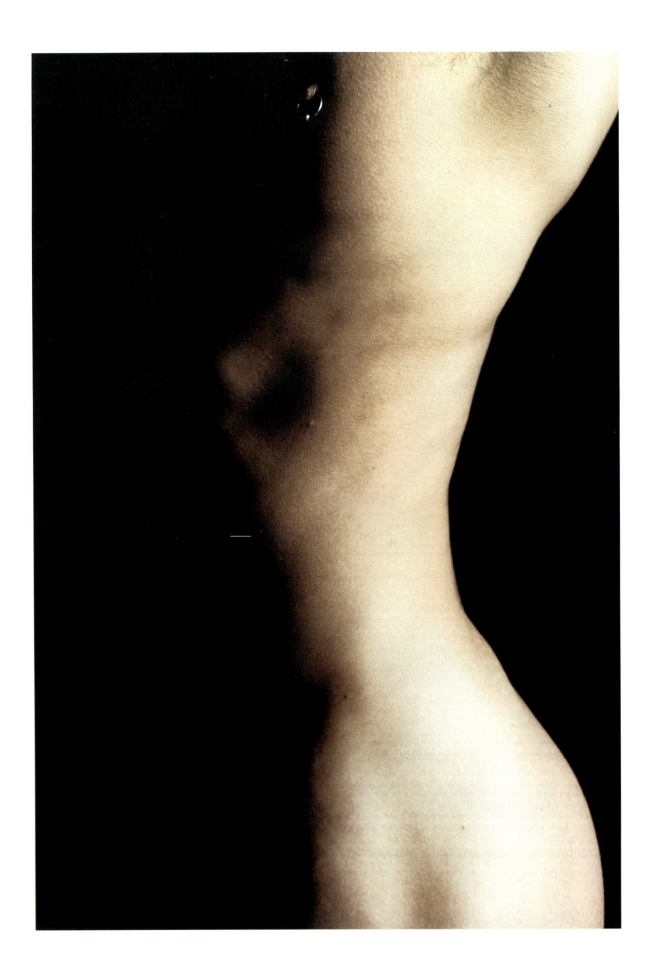

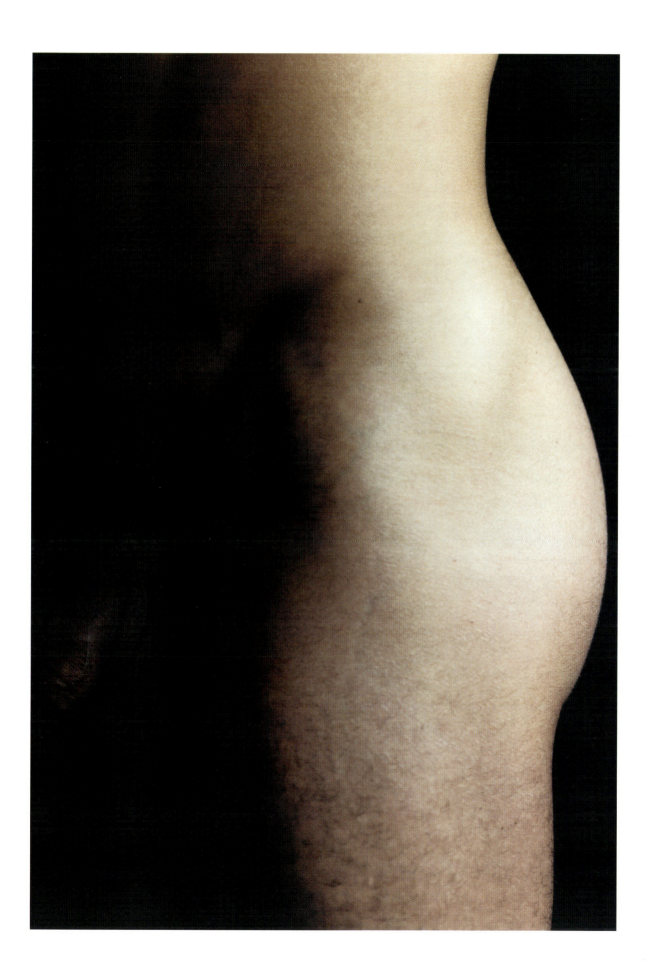

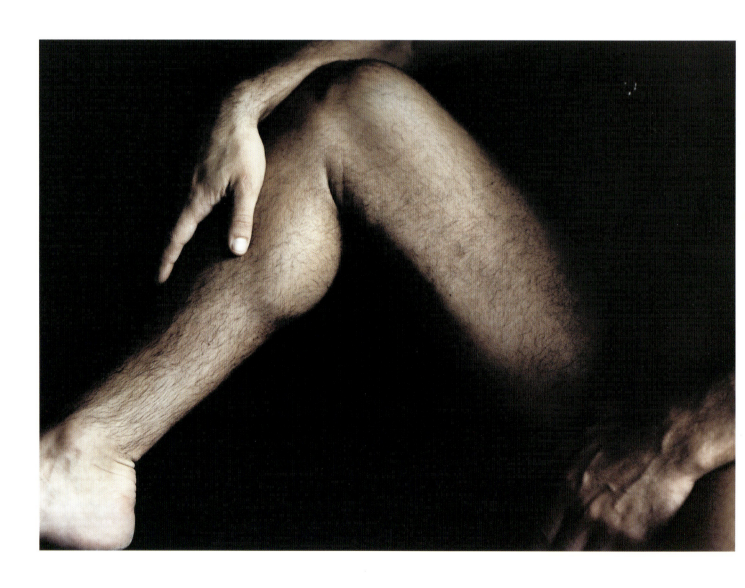

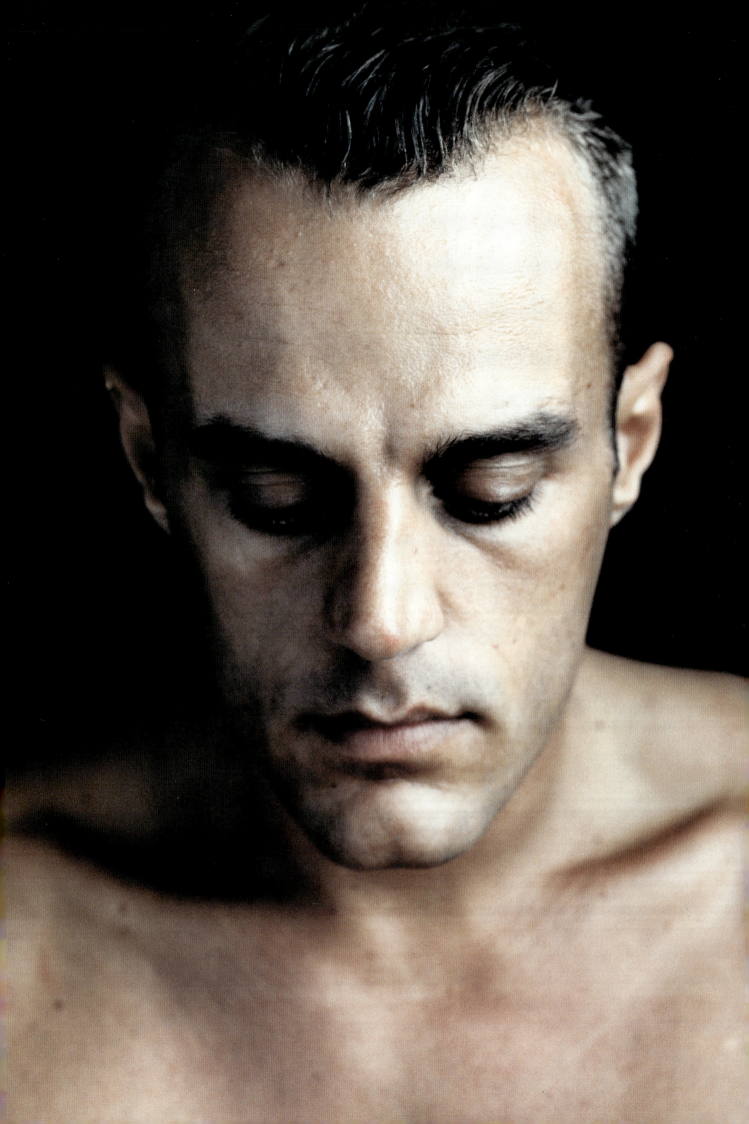

Ich möchte meiner Mutter danken, die mir mit ihrer Toleranz den Weg geebnet hat.

I would like to thank my mother, whose tolerance paved the way for me.